A Sticker Story™

Spin Around the Birthday Planet

Mary Blocksma and Sherry Long

Illustrated by Jane Dyer

Developed by The Hampton-Brown Company, Inc.

HPBooks

About Your Sticker Story™ Book

Here is a book children can read and have fun with again and again. Children participate in the story by adding stickers to pictures as the adventure unfolds. To begin, tear out the page of stickers near the front of the book. As children read the book, they will find flip-ups at the bottom of different pages. These flip-ups tell the child which sticker to select from the sticker page and where to place it in the picture. After reading the story, stickers can be removed from pictures and placed on the storage page near the front of the book. Stickers can be removed from that page to provide hours of fun each time the book is read.

Your Sticker Story™ is educational, too! Applying stickers gives children practice in comprehension as they match pictures to text. The vocabulary used in the story reinforces important words children are learning to read in school. Over 80% of the words in the story are commonly taught by the end of first grade.

Published by HPBooks
P.O. Box 5367
Tucson, AZ 85703
(602) 888-2150

For HPBooks:
Publishers: Bill and Helen Fisher
Executive Editor: Rick Bailey
Editorial Director: Randy Summerlin
Art Director: Don Burton

For The Hampton-Brown Company, Inc.:
Project Editor: Elisabeth Meyer Wechsler
Designer: John Edeen

ISBN: 0-89586-202-6

Turn the page and let's get started!

Jenny and Zip went down the hall
to Roger's. They rang the bell.
Then they waited and waited.

At last, Roger opened the door.

"Let's go out and play," said Zip.

"I don't want to," said Roger.
"My mom and dad forgot my birthday."

"You didn't tell us today was
your birthday," said Zip.

"We have to find you a present,"
said Jenny. "Come on, Roger. We can
start looking in the park."

"Well," said Roger. "I guess
that's better than nothing."

The children walked to the park.

"Don't be sad, Roger," said Jenny.
"We think you're out of this world."

"Right," said Zip. "That's why we
have to find your present in outer space.
Look, there's our spaceship now!"

"It's just a merry-go-round,"
said Roger.

"Look again," said Jenny. "It's
a spaceship."

**Use a
sticker to turn the
merry-go-round into a spaceship.**

Zip and Jenny pulled Roger over to the spaceship. They made Roger get in first. Soon the spaceship began to spin.

"Where are we?" asked Zip.

"We can't be very high," said Roger. "I can see a balloon over there."

"That's the Birthday Planet," said Jenny. "That's where we're going."

Use a sticker to turn the balloon into the Birthday Planet.

Soon the spaceship landed.

"Look!" said Zip. "It IS the Birthday Planet."

"I can see space flowers," said Jenny.

Roger began to feel happier. "This IS fun," he said.

The children jumped out. Roger began to gasp. "I can't get enough air," he said.

"I am turning blue," said Jenny.

"Me, too," said Zip. "We need space suits!"

Use a sticker to help the kids out. Give them each a space suit.

"Look at us now!" cried Jenny.
"We're dressed for the planet after
all. Let's go!"

The children began looking
around the planet.

Zip found some tall space
flowers. "Here, Roger," he said.
"These are for your birthday."

"Just looking at those flowers
makes me sneeze!" cried Roger.
"ACHOOOOOOO!"

"I guess space flowers aren't
a good present," said Zip sadly.

Roger saw a big rock under the slide. "Let's take that rock back," he said. "Rocks can help us learn about planets."

"That's not a rock," said Jenny. "That's a big jewel!"

"A space jewel," said Zip.

Use a
sticker to turn
the rock into a space jewel.

The jewel was so bright that
it hurt Jenny's eyes. She put her
arm over her eyes and stepped back.
"Look out, Jenny!" cried Roger.
But it was too late. Jenny fell
right into a big crater!

Roger and Zip ran over and looked down.

"I'm okay," said Jenny. "But I need some jet shoes to get out of here."

"Maybe those sand pails would help," said Roger.

"They look just like jet shoes to ME!" said Zip.

Use a sticker to turn the sand pails into jet shoes.

Roger tossed the jet shoes into
the crater. Jenny put them on. Soon
she flew to the top.

"I'm glad to be out of there," she said. "Now let's get that space jewel for Roger."

"For ME?" said Roger. "Oh, boy!"

"Not so fast," said Zip. "What about that space creature?"

Use a sticker to turn the slide into a space creature.

Jenny looked at the space creature. Then she looked hard at Zip. "We can get that jewel for our best friend, can't we, Zip?" said Jenny.

"But the space creature will get me!" cried Zip.

"No, Zip. You just have to make it sneeze," said Jenny. "Here, put these space flowers under its nose."

Slowly, Zip walked up to the
creature. He put the flowers right
under its nose.

"ACHOOOOOOO!" sneezed the
creature. "ACHOOOOOOO!"

Roger and Jenny ran to get the
jewel. "Hurry," cried Jenny. "It
might stop sneezing!"

Just then, the creature DID stop!

"Look what you did, Zip,"
laughed Roger. "Your space flowers
turned the creature into a slide!"

**Use a
sticker to turn the
space creature back into a slide.**

The children ran to their
spaceship. Just then, Roger saw
something coming at them.

"Look out!" cried Roger. "It's
a rocket!"

"Is it full of robots?" asked Zip.

"Yes, and they want the space
jewel!" cried Jenny.

"Maybe robots sneeze, too,"
said Zip.

"Robots NEVER sneeze!" said
Roger. "We're in trouble now. Let's
get out of here."

Use a sticker to help the kids out. Turn the rocket into a kite.

The children jumped into their spaceship and took off.

"Look," said Zip. "The Birthday Planet is getting smaller and smaller."

"Now it looks like a balloon!" said Jenny.

**Use a
sticker to turn the
Birthday Planet back into a balloon.**

The spaceship landed in the
park. Zip, Jenny, and Roger got
out. They took off their space
suits and put them into the spaceship.

"Do I have to take off my jet
shoes, too?" asked Jenny.

"Yes," said Roger. "We'll use them
on the next trip."

"Maybe not," said Zip. "Our
spaceship looks like a merry-go-round
now."

**Use a
sticker to turn the
spaceship back into a merry-go-round.**

The children walked home with the space jewel. On the way, Roger said, "Thank you, Jenny and Zip. This is the best birthday I ever had!"

"Even if your mom and dad forgot?" asked Jenny.

"I guess so," said Roger.

Zip began to laugh, but Roger didn't know why.

"Shhhh!" said Jenny.

The children got to Roger's door.
Jenny opened it slowly. The room
was full of children!

"SURPRISE!" cried everyone.

"Happy Birthday, Roger!" said
his dad.

"What a pretty rock," said his mom.

"We got it on the Birthday Planet,"
said Zip.

Roger was too surprised to talk.

"We had to get you out of here so your mom and dad could surprise you," said Jenny.

"Now you have REAL presents," said Zip.

Roger put the space jewel on top of all the presents. "I like the jewel best because it's out of this world," he laughed. "Just like my birthday!"